GUNNER,
FOOTBALL HERO

JAMES E. RANSOME

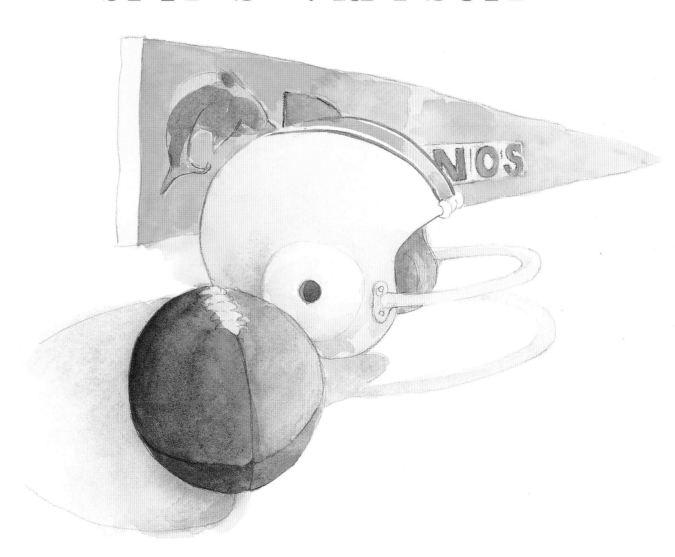

Holiday House / New York

Library of Congress Cataloging-in-Publication Data
Ransome, James.
Gunner, football hero / by James E. Ransome. — 1st ed.
p. cm.
Summary: When short, round Gunner, the third-string quarterback,
finally gets to play in a big game, everyone treats him like a hero.
ISBN 978-0-8234-2053-7 (hardcover)
[1. Football—Fiction.] I. Title.
PZ7.R1755Gu 2009
[E]—dc22
2008048487

To Mort Drucker, Jack Davis, Don Martin,
and all the other artists at MAD magazine
who inspired me to draw.

Gunner was a great name
for a boy who wanted to play football.
Gunner didn't look like most football players.
He was too short and too round.

Gunner was the only child of Mr. and Mrs. Smith.
The Smiths did not care for sports,
but they knew how much Gunner loved football.

They watched him practice every day before and after school.
They made sure he was the first in line
to sign up for the town's PeeWee team.

Gunner told his coaches that he wanted to play quarterback.
His coaches and teammates laughed.
Once Gunner threw a pass, their laughter stopped.

"Okay," the coach said.
"Gunner, you're our third-string quarterback."

Once the football season began,
Gunner never got a chance to play.
He sat on the bench for every game.
But he was always the first to arrive
and the last to leave practice.
On Saturdays he watched college football
and on Sundays, the pros.
After school Gunner would study his playbook.
But in game after game,
Gunner sat on the bench.

In the last game of the season,
the Malden Tigers were up against the Woodland Bobcats
in the PeeWee championship called the Mighty Bowl.
The Tigers were down by two touchdowns.
And in the last quarter, someone's cleats
landed on the first-string quarterback's hand.
His parents took him to the hospital.

On the very next play, the second-string quarterback
was sacked so hard he saw stars.
His mommy took him home.

"Gunner, you're in," shouted the coach.
All the Tigers fans sighed.

Gunner was sacked when he ran the wrong way
on his first play in the game.
The Tigers fans booed.
"HANG IN THERE, SON!" yelled his parents.

But the Tigers fans cheered
when Gunner threw
a straight-as-an-arrow spiral to his wide receiver
and scored his first touchdown.

The Malden Tigers defense stopped the Woodland Bobcats.
The ball went back to the Tigers with three minutes on the clock.
The Tigers sideline was quiet when Gunner ran onto the field,

except for a "GO, GUNNER" from his parents.

Then Gunner threw a long bomb to the tight end
for his second touchdown to tie the game.
Everyone on the Malden Tigers side of the field CHEERED!

The next page went:

Where's my cow?

Is that my cow?

It goes, "Hruuugh!"

It is a hippopotamus!

That's not my cow!

Sam Vimes liked doing the Hruuugh!
But he said to himself: This is
getting daft! This is no way
to find your cow!

So he said to young Sam: "If you lose your cow you should report this to the Watch under the Domestic & Farmyard Animals (Lost) Act of 1809. They will swing into action with keenness and speed. Your cow will be found. If it has been impersonating other animals, it may be arrested. If you are a stupid person, do not look for your cow yourself. Never try to milk a chicken. It hardly ever works."

Young Sam thought this was funny.

And Sam Vimes thought: Why is Young Sam's nursery full of farmyard animals, anyway? Why are his books full of moo-cows and baa-lambs? He is growing up in a city. He will only see them on a plate! They go *sizzle!*

I can think of a more useful book. A book with streets in it, not fields. A book about the place where he'll grow up.

He tried it the very next night.

It went:

Where's my daddy?

Is that my daddy?

It goes, "Bugrit!

Millennium Hand and Shrimp!"

It is Foul Ole Ron!

That's not my daddy!

Young Sam laughed.

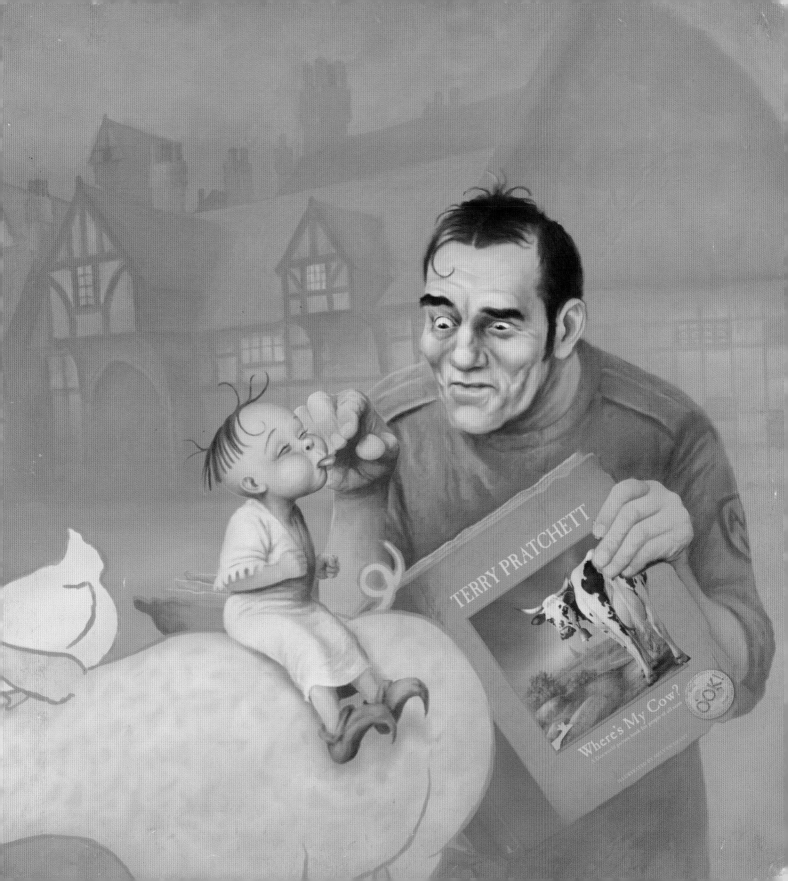

So Sam Vimes went on:

Where's my daddy?

Is that my daddy?

It goes, "Haaaaak! Gack! Ptui!"

It is Coffin' Henry!

That's not my daddy!

Young Sam said, "Ptui!"

Where's my daddy? [Sam Vimes read]

Is that my daddy?

It goes, "That's cutting me own throat!"

It is Cut-Me-Own-Throat Dibbler!

Don't eat his pies!

Young Sam yelled, "Fwoat!"

That's not my daddy! [read Vimes]

Where's my daddy?

Is that my daddy?

It goes, "I fink, derefore I am. I fink."

It is Sergeant Detritus the troll!

That's not my daddy!

"Fink!" shouted Young Sam,

red in the face with laughter.

Sam Vimes was leaping around now.

Where's my daddy?

Is that my daddy?

It goes, "Don't let me detain you."

It is Lord Vetinari! He rules the city!

Really don't let him detain you!

That's not my daddy!

Where's my daddy?

Is that my daddy?

It goes—

"I heard the noise. Is everything all right, dear?"

Sam and Young Sam looked at the doorway. There was Lady Sybil, Young Sam's mummy. She looked worried. She also looked a bit suspicious.

"Er, fine, dear," said Sam Vimes.

"You're not getting him over-excited, are you, dear?" said Lady Sybil.

"Just reading him his book, dear," said Sam Vimes.

"Ptui!" laughed Young Sam. "Buglit!"

Very quickly, Sam Vimes read:

"'Where's my cow?

Is that my cow?

It goes: "Hissss!"

It is a goose.

That's not my cow.'"

"Very well, then," said Lady Sybil, and went downstairs.

When he heard the door close, Sam Vimes leaned over the cot and whispered, "Where's my daddy? Is that my daddy? It goes: 'I arrest you in the name of the Law!' *That*'s my daddy!"

"Law," yawned Young Sam, falling asleep.

"That's my boy," said Sam Vimes, as he tucked him in.

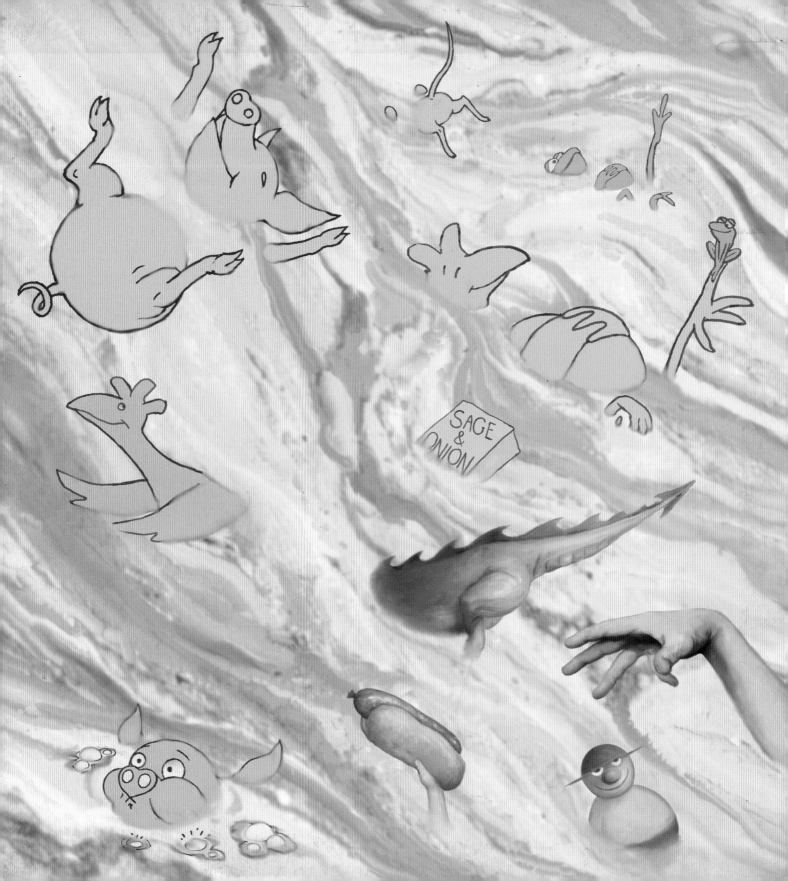